To my mum, Ella Grey, and my dad, Peter Grey

Many thanks to KIM for consenting to a guest appearance.

The author and the publishers would like to thank the Reader's Digest Association, Ltd.,
for permission to reprint an extract from the *Encyclopedia of Garden Plants and Flowers* © 1997.

THIS IS A BORZOI BOOK PUBLISHED BY ALFRED A. KNOPF

Copyright © 2003 by Mini Grey

www.randomhouse.com/kids

Library of Congress Cataloging-in-Publication Data
Grey, Mini.
The very smart pea and the princess-to-be / by Mini Grey.
p.   cm.
SUMMARY: The pea gives its own version of what happened in the fairy tale "The Princess and the Pea,"
from the time of its birth in the Palace Garden until it helps arrange a royal marriage.
ISBN 0-375-82626-2 (trade) — ISBN 0-375-92626-7 (lib. bdg.)
[1. Peas—Fiction. 2. Princesses—Fiction.] I. Title.
PZ7.G873 Ve 2003   [E]—dc21   2002152879

MANUFACTURED IN MALAYSIA
September 2003
10 9 8 7 6 5 4 3 2 1

The
VERY SMART PEA
and the
PRINCESS-TO-BE

MiNi GREY

ALFRED A. KNOPF   NEW YORK

Many years ago, I was born in the Palace Garden,
among rows of carrots and beets and cabbages.

I nestled snugly in a velvety pod with my brothers and sisters.
I felt a tingle. I knew that somehow I would be important.

WAYS WITH PEAS

Pea and Raspberry Jelly

Ingredients:

Fresh Peas
Butter
Raspberr...

Method:
Shell p...
boilin...
Mak...
b...

WAYS W...

Petits Pois Su...

Ingredients:

Fresh Peas
Butter
Little Biscuits
Vanilla Ice-cream

Method:
...ll the peas and simmer unt...
...ling water. Add a knob...
...two scoops of ice-cre...
...p. Pour over the h...

The time came for us to go to the Palace Kitchen. We were shelled and put in a bowl. We were going to be part of a New Recipe. Then, suddenly, I was picked from the pile! I was put in a little box, with soft tissue to protect me from bruising. And I was taken by the Queen.

PEAS
la Mode

At this point in my story, I'm going to have to give you some background information. Let's start with the Queen.

A year earlier, before I even started to grow on my pea plant, the Queen had been nagging her son. "You are nearly thirty-four years old, Prince!" she said. "It really is high time you married. The Public expects it. Your Kingdom demands it. And if you are not married within one year, I shall stop your allowance."

The Prince got quite a large allowance, and he really didn't want it to be taken away.

"I'll start looking for a bride immediately, Mother," he answered.

And the search began.

The Prince traveled the Known World. He met princesses of all shapes and sizes, with a wide range of hobbies and interests.

But none of them seemed like a Real Princess.
Somehow they were not right for him.

After a year's search, the Prince
returned home, feeling glum.
"THAT'S ENOUGH!" shouted
the Queen. She stormed off to the
Palace Kitchen. She came back with
me. In my little box. "Now," said the
Queen, "listen carefully. This
is something only
queens know.

'A Real Princess will be able to feel this little pea as she sleeps, even if she is sleeping on top of twenty mattresses and feather beds. And you are going to marry the first girl who can feel this pea!"

Months passed. I spent most nights in the darkness under
a pile of twenty mattresses and feather beds and a princess.

In the morning, the Queen would ask,
"And how did you sleep, my dear?"
The princesses had been properly brought up.
They always answered politely:
"Like a log, thank you, Ma'am," or
"Like a baby, thank you, Ma'am,"
and they all said:
"WHAT a comfortable bed!"
They were, as I said, all very polite
princesses.
"The Prince will never find his
princess at this rate," I thought
to myself. "I must help.
Somehow."

One night, a furious storm raged.
Rain lashed the Palace. Thunderclaps shook the walls.
Lightning flashed through the window panes.
There was a little knock on the Palace door.
A small, wet person stood on the doormat.

"Could THIS be the Real Princess?" gasped the Queen.

Before she could say a word, the small,
wet person was put to bed on top
of the twenty mattresses and feather beds.
With me, of course, underneath.
In the darkness under the mattresses,
I recognized the soft snoring.
It was my gardener!
"I must help," I thought.
I tried jiggling and wriggling.
The snoring continued quietly.
"I must do something!" I thought.
I inched my way to the edge.
And then I started to climb. Slowly I
struggled to the top of the towering pile.
I softly rolled across the pillow, right to the
girl's ear. "There is something Large
and Round and very Uncomfortable in
the bed under you," I whispered.
And while she slept, I told her about
the Large Round Uncomfortable
thing for three hours.

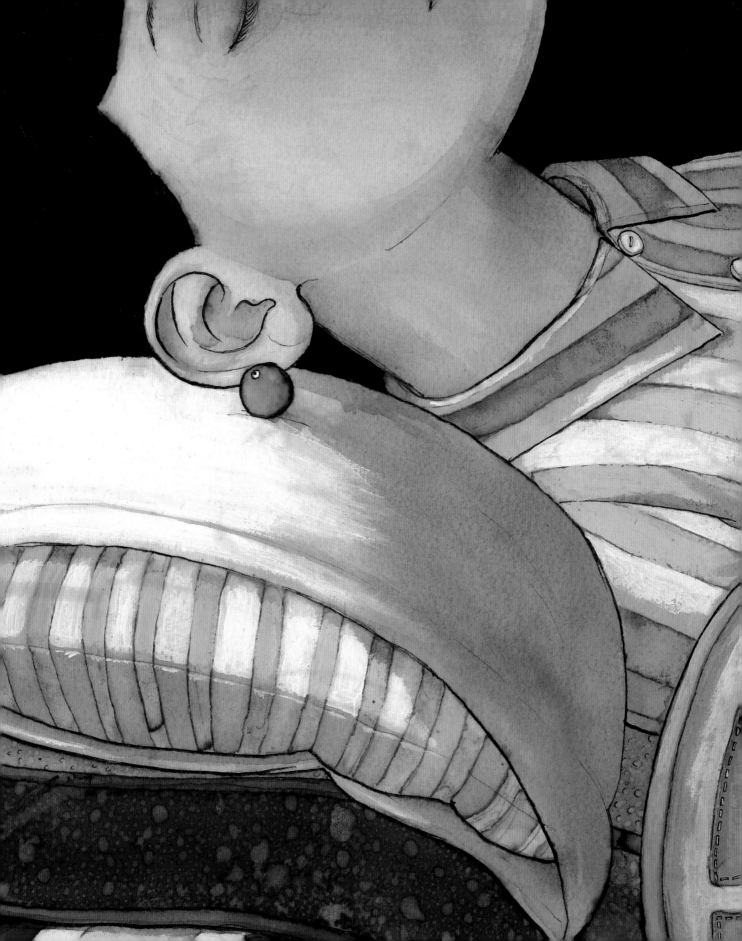

In the morning, the Queen asked
the girl how she had slept.
"Oh, it was awful!" she sighed.
"Something Large and Round and
Uncomfortable was bothering me
all night."
The Queen was delighted to
hear this.

exhibit 235582

The wedding was lovely.
The Queen was interested to meet the new Princess's parents.
And I'm sure they will all live together happily ever after.

And as for me? I became a Very Important Artifact.
And I now have my own glass case. I am On Display.
And if you visit the right museum and look in the right place,
you may chance to see me.

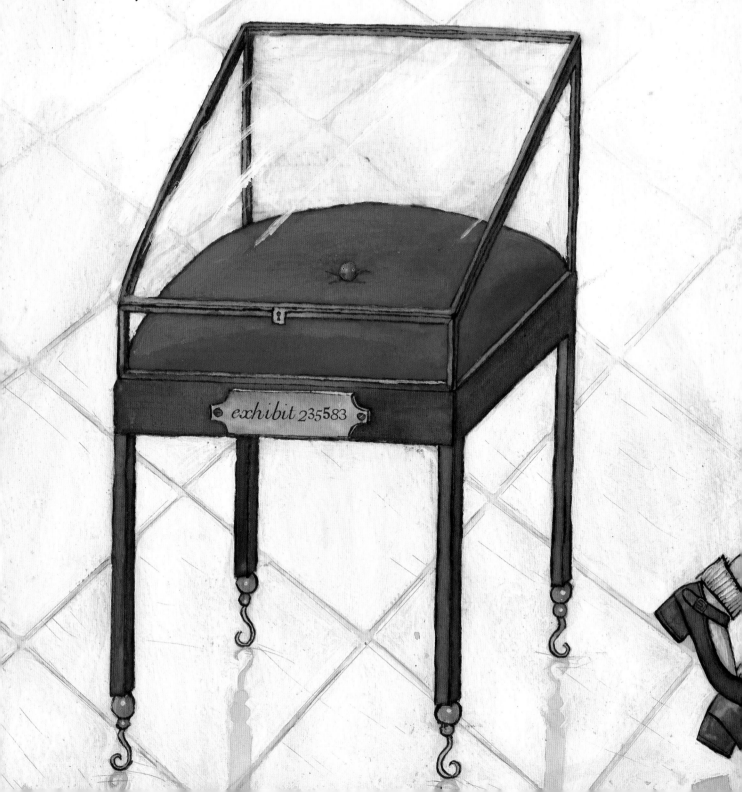

exhibit 235583